TONY BALONEY
School Rules

BY
PAM MUÑOZ RYAN

ILLUSTRATED BY
EDWIN FOTHERINGHAM

SCHOLASTIC INC.

To Yonatan and Elad —P.M.R.

To my family: Becky, Anna, and Joe —E.F.

Text copyright © 2012
by Pam Muñoz Ryan
Illustrations copyright © 2012
by Edwin Fotheringham

LIBRARY OF CONGRESS CATALOGING-IN-
PUBLICATION DATA AVAILABLE

ISBN 978-0-545-48167-0
12 11 10 9 8 7 6 5 4 3 2
12 13 14 15 16
Printed in the U.S.A.   40
First Scholastic paperback printing,
September 2012

The text in this book was set in Adobe
Caslon Pro Regular. The display type was
set in P22 Kane. The title was hand lettered
by Edwin Fotheringham. The illustrations
were created using digital media.
Book design by Marijka Kostiw

CONTENTS

4

THE BIG DAY

Tony Baloney,

the macaroni penguin,

wakes up early.

Before Poppa Baloney can

remind him, he dresses,

then brushes his teeth.

He's ready!

5

Today he won't have to obey
Bossy Big Sister Baloney.
He won't have to play with the
Bothersome Babies Baloney.
Today he is going to school!

6

He packs his backpack

with his favorite things:

Parmesan cheese,

Little Green Walrus Guys, and . . .

7

. . . his very best

stuffed animal buddy, Dandelion.

I'm a teeny-weeny bit worried about the big day.

I know. Big Sister says there are a lot of rules. But Momma says we will be *just fine.*

8

What if I get lost on the way to the bathroom? What if I don't find a place to sit at lunchtime? What if I can't follow the rules?

Don't worry, we can do it. I'll be there if you need me.

Besides, would you rather stay home with the Bothersome Babies?

Let's see . . . Drool or school? Pack my pencils!

9

At breakfast, Big Sister Baloney

tells Tony Baloney twenty times,

or maybe twice, that she was in

Mrs. Gamboney's class too.

"I was her most perfect student."

"Bee Bee, we don't have

to be perfect," says Momma Baloney.

"We just have to do our best."

10

"Well, *I* was Line Leader

the first day," she says.

"Maybe I will be Line Leader

the first day too," says Tony Baloney.

"Fat chance!" says Big Sister Baloney.

Tony Baloney does not love trouble . . .

. . . but trouble loves him.

12

SCHOOL RULES

At school, Big Sister Baloney walks
Tony Baloney to his classroom.
"Dandelion must stay in your cubby,"
she says. "It's a rule. Be a rule-keeper.
That's my motto."
"That's my motto too," says Tony Baloney.

"Welcome to Mrs. G's Garden!"

says Mrs. Gamboney.

She is smiley.

Her voice is cheerful.

She smells like peaches and coconut.

Mrs. Gamboney grins at Tony Baloney.

"You must be Bee Bee's brother!

She loved to be my Line Leader."

Tony Baloney grins back and thinks,

I would love to be Line Leader too.

15

Mrs. Gamboney points to the board.

"These are our classroom rules."

She reads them aloud:

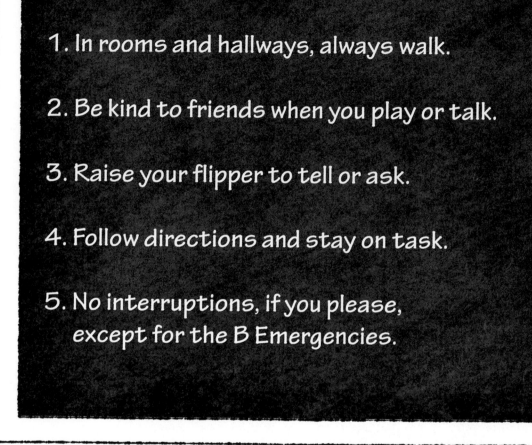

1. In rooms and hallways, always walk.

2. Be kind to friends when you play or talk.

3. Raise your flipper to tell or ask.

4. Follow directions and stay on task.

5. No interruptions, if you please,
   except for the B Emergencies.

"Does everyone know what

the B Emergencies are?"

No one knows.

Mrs. Gamboney explains.

"B Emergencies are:

Bathroom, Bandage, and Belly-upset.

When I am working with other penguins,

you may interrupt me *only*

if you need to use the *bathroom*,

or need a *bandage*,

or someone has a *belly-upset*.

Does everyone know what

belly-upset means?"

Tony Baloney knows.

19

"It means *barf*!" he shouts.

Tony Baloney and Bob laugh.

Everyone else laughs too.

Soon the class is a mess

of giggling penguins.

20

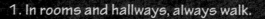

1. In rooms and hallways, always walk.

2. Be kind to friends when you play or t

3. Raise your flipper to tell or ask.

4. Follow directions a   ay on t

5. No interruptions, if you
   except for the B Emergen

Mrs. Gamboney points to rule number three

and asks everyone to *please* settle down.

21

JAMES COOK ELEMENTARY

22

At recess, all the penguins
play freeze tag. Tony Baloney
is so excited that he accidentally
tags Bob too hard.

Mrs. Gamboney frowns.
"Tony Baloney, please remember
to be kind to your friends."

At lunch, Tony Baloney carries his tray

across the Everything Room.

He wants to sit with Bob.

When he sees a spot

next to him, he runs.

Mrs. Gamboney calls,

"Tony Baloney, *always walk . . .*"

But it is too late.

Slip. Slide. Crash!

25

After lunch, Tony Baloney needs
a moment with Dandelion.

And then Mrs. Gamboney had a little
talk with me about the rules. She said
that I'll get the hang of them soon.
And she said we shouldn't let these
small, or maybe gigantic, disasters spoil
an otherwise lovely beginning of the
school year. Oh, and I'm not Line Leader.

26

B EMERGENCIES

That afternoon,

the penguins take turns

working with Mrs. Gamboney.

While they wait,

they have Choice Time.

Tony Baloney chooses blocks.

He and Bob build a tall tower . . .

. . . but then seven,

or maybe seventy-seven,

blocks fall on top of Bob.

"Mrs. Gamboney!" calls Tony Baloney.

Without looking up, Mrs. Gamboney asks,

"Tony Baloney, is this a B Emergency?"

Tony Baloney thinks about the rules:

bathroom, bandage, belly-upset.

"No," he says and wonders what to do . . .

. . . until he realizes this *is* a B Emergency.

He bellows:

TONY

32

"Bob is buried beneath the blocks!"

FRIENDSHIP AMBASSADOR

"Today Tony Baloney is our

Friendship Ambassador," says Mrs. Gamboney.

"Does everyone know what that means?"

"It means he's a good friend," says Sally,

"especially to Bob."

34

"That's right," says Mrs. Gamboney.

"Now we need to add to our list of

B Emergencies. Does anyone have ideas?"

Everyone does.

B Emergencies

1. Bathroom
2. Bandage
3. Belly-upset
4. Buried Beneath Blocks
5. Bruised Beak
6. Barking Beetles
7. Baboons on Bicycles
8. Boomerangs
9. Banana Bombs

Soon the class is a mess

of giggling penguins.

That night at dinner, Momma Baloney says,

"Wow. Friendship Ambassador!"

"Very impressive," says Poppa Baloney.

"And on the first day," says Tony Baloney.

Big Sister Baloney says, "It's not
polite to wear a hat at the table."
"He may leave it on," says Momma Baloney.
And he does.

School was fun. I made a friend named Bob.

I liked it too. I met a stuffed turtle named Pedro.

Mrs. Gamboney is nice.

I kind of love her.

Did I tell you that I'm Friendship Ambassador?

Twice, or maybe fifty times. But tell me again and I'll pretend to be surprised.